MATT PHELAN

LEAVE IT TO PLUM!

Greenwillow Books

An Imprint of HarperCollinsPublishers

Leave It to Plum!
Text and illustrations copyright © 2022 by Matt Phelan
All rights reserved. No part of this book may be used or reproduced in any manner whatsoever without written permission except in the case of brief quotations embodied in critical articles and reviews. Printed in the United States of America. For information address HarperCollins Children's Books, a division of HarperCollins Publishers, 195 Broadway, New York, NY 10007.
www.harpercollinschildrens.com
The text of this book is set in Charlotte Book.
Book design by Sylvie Le Floc'h

Library of Congress Cataloging-in-Publication Data

Names: Phelan, Matt, writer, illustrator.
Title: Leave it to Plum! / written and illustrated by Matt Phelan.
Description: First edition. I New York : Greenwillow Books, an Imprint of HarperCollins
    Publishers, [2022] I Audience: Ages 8–12 I Audience: Grades 4–6 I Summary: Every day
    at the Athensville Zoo the peacocks are allowed to wander freely among the visitors,
    delighting and guiding kids and grownups alike, and kind, curious Plum is the peacock
    most proud of their responsibility.
Identifiers: LCCN 2021055304 (print) I LCCN 2021055305 (ebook) I ISBN 9780063079168
    (hardcover) I ISBN 9780063079199 (ebook) I ISBN 9780063079182 (paperback)
Subjects: CYAC: Peacocks—Fiction. I Zoos—Fiction. I Humorous stories. I LCGFT: Animal
    fiction. I Humorous fiction.
Classification: LCC PZ7.P44882 Le 2022   (print) I LCC PZ7.P44882   (ebook) I DDC
    [Fic]—dc23
LC record available at https://lccn.loc.gov/2021055304
LC ebook record available at https://lccn.loc.gov/2021055305

23 24 25 26 27 LBC 6 5 4 3 2
First Greenwillow paperback edition, 2023
Greenwillow Books

For all of my friends in Athensville

Entrance

Habitrail

Monorail (Closed)

1. The Great Tree
2. Statue of Plato
3. Small & Unusual Mammals
4. Reptiles & Amphibians
5. Lagoon
6. Bears
7. Rhinoceroses, Zebras, & Giraffes
8. Elephants
9. Temporary Pen
10. The Outback
11. Mammals
12. Aviary
13. Prairie Dogs
14. Flamingos, Penguins, & Ducks
15. Carousel
16. Big Cats
17. Snack Shack
18. Primates
19. Hippopotamuses
20. Otters
21. Monkeys & Memories
22. Zoovenirs
23–25. Keeper Buildings

MAP OF THE
ATHENSVILLE ZOO

Chapter One
**Welcome to
the Athensville Zoo**

It was a fine, crisp morning at the Athensville Zoo. A peacock and an alligator were in the middle of a staring contest.

"You blinked," said the small peacock named Plum.

"I haven't blinked since Tuesday," said the large alligator named Mike.

They stared.

And stared.

And stared.

"Do you know why I will win, Plum?" asked Mike.

"You won't win this time," said Plum.

"I will, because you cannot sit still for very long."

"I'm a peppy, purple peacock!" piped Plum. "Try saying *that* three times fast."

Mike paused, then he said: "Peppy Purple Peacock, Peppy Purple Peacock, Purpy Pebble Pep—oh, drat!" And Mike blinked.

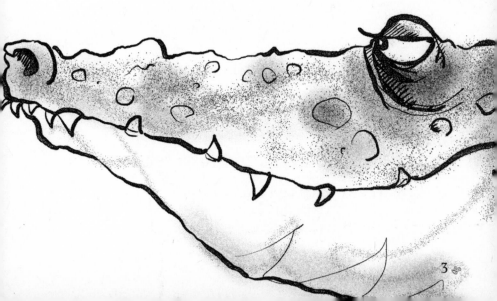

"I win!" Plum shouted.

"The zoo is about to open, Plum," said Mike. "You better get moving."

"See you later, alligator!" said Plum. Mike was quiet. Plum leaned in. He leaned in farther, one wing pointed at Mike.

"No," said Mike.

"Say it. *Please?*" pleaded Plum.

Mike sighed. "After the clock . . . how does it go again?"

"After the clock tick tocks . . ." sang Plum.

"After the clock tick tocks, peacock," Mike mumbled as he slid into his lagoon.

Plum cheered. "I think that saying is really catching on, Mike," he called.

Bubbles rose to the surface of the lagoon.

"Thank you!" said Plum.

The peacock zipped away down the path, greeting all of the zoo animals he passed. All waved wings, arms, legs, trunks, or tails back at Plum.

Why was he walking through the zoo as he pleased, you ask? Did he not belong in a peacock pen of some sort? Well, the answer goes way back to the beginning of the Athensville Zoo. Henrietta "Henny" Grange, founder of the zoo, loved peacocks. Her pet peacock, Plato, was permitted to wander the zoo freely and became a great favorite of all visitors.

This tradition continued with a whole flock of free-range peacocks, including Plato's great-great-great-great-grand-peachick, Plum. The peacocks served as the official ambassadors to the zoo guests. Their duties were as follows:

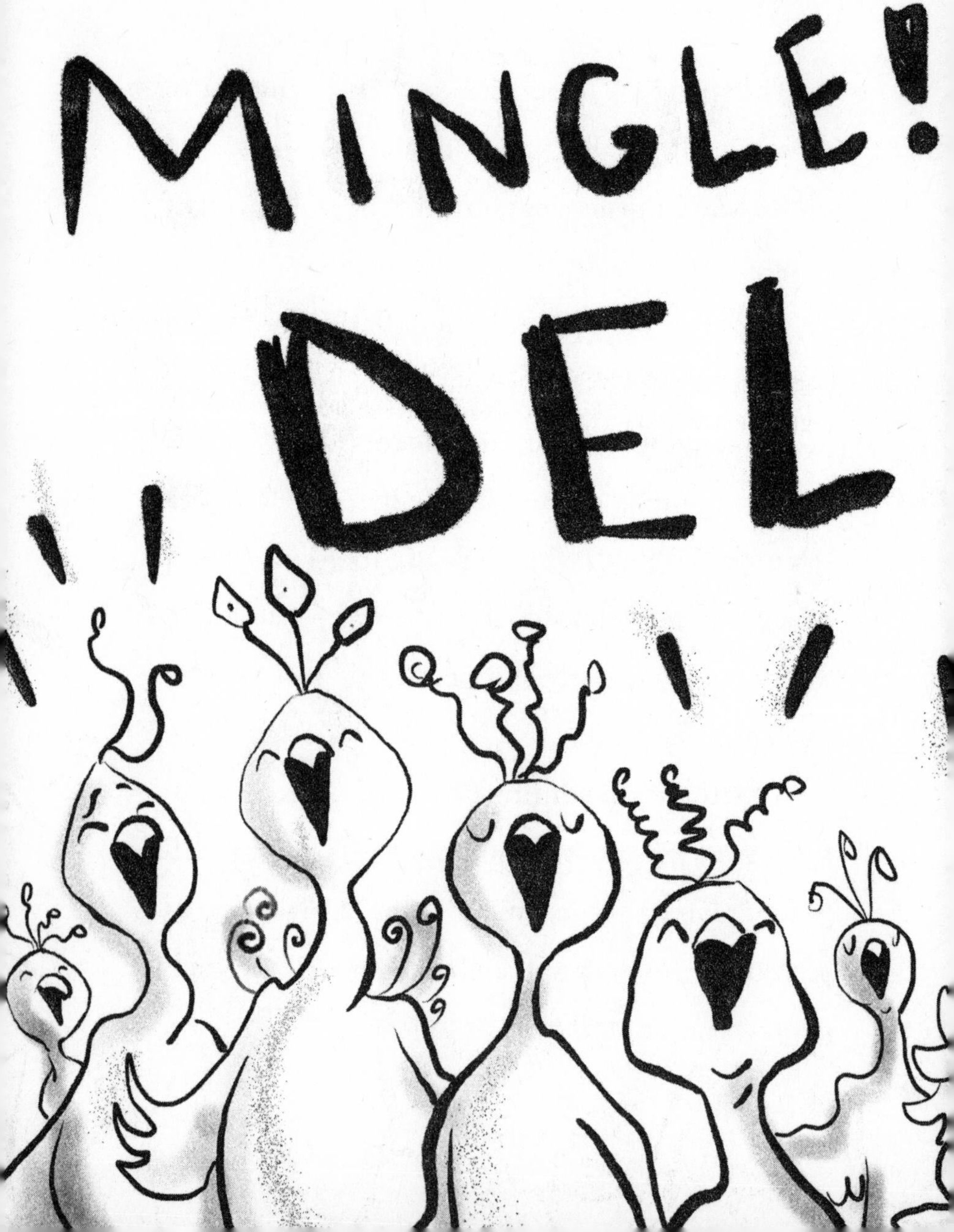
MINGLE!
DEL

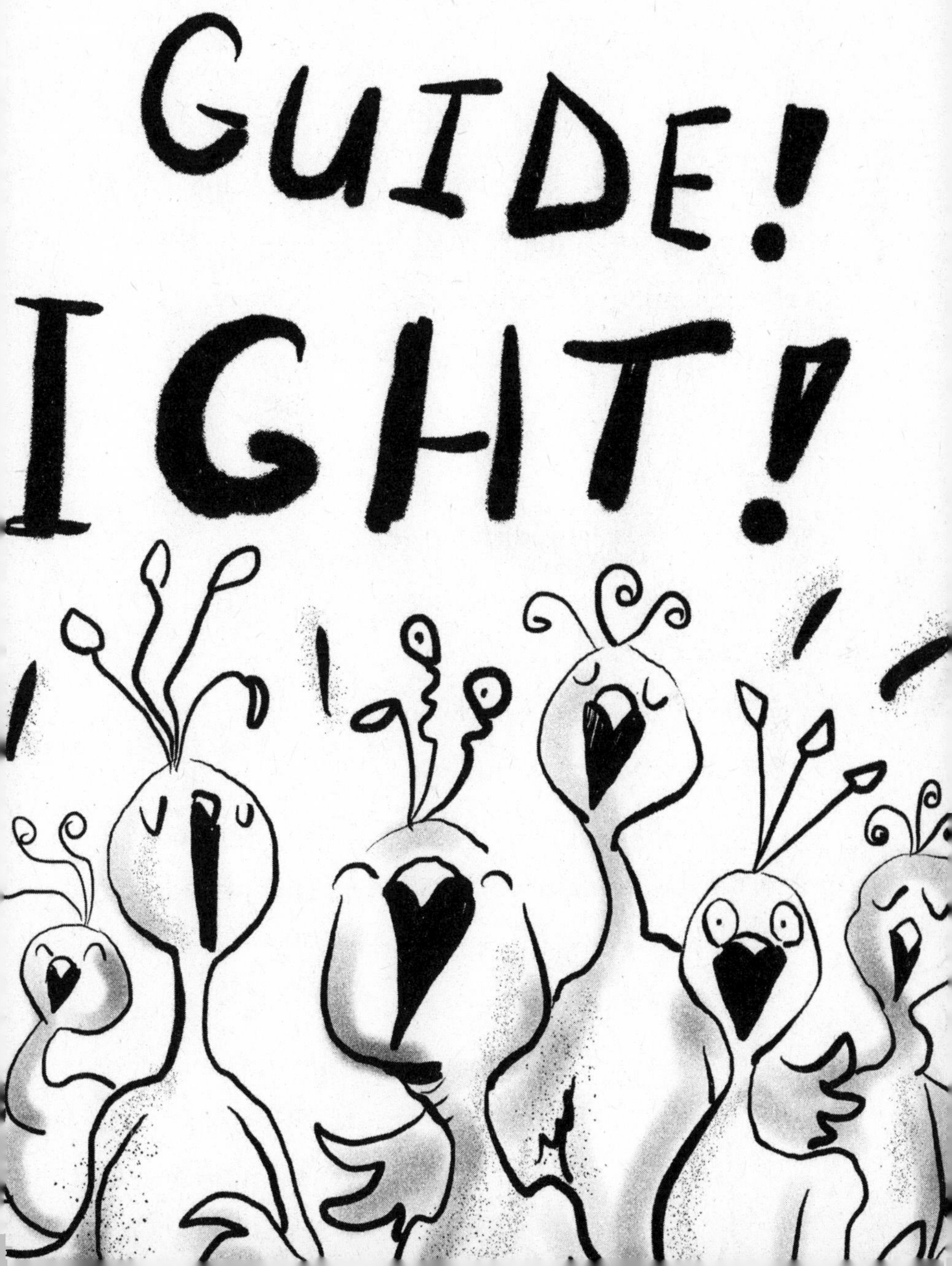
GUIDE!
IGHT!

Every morning the ambassadors met for the Mandatory Morning Meeting of Athensville Zoo Peacocks. As today's meeting came to order, Hampstead, the head peacock, stood as usual under the Great Tree. All peacocks were in attendance.

All but one.

"PLUM!" bellowed Hampstead.

Plum skidded around the path and joined the congregation.

"Here, O Great Leader!" shouted Plum. "Bright-eyed and feathery tailed!"

"Kind of you to join us for the *Mandatory* Morning Meeting, Plum," grumbled Hampstead.

"Wouldn't miss it!" piped Plum.

Meg, a young peafowl, smiled at Plum. "One of these days you'll make it on time," she whispered.

"One of these days." Plum grinned.

Hampstead ruffled his feathers and continued.

"We, the peafowl of the Athensville Zoo, have served since the beginning as ambassadors to the zoo's esteemed guests. Our duties are sacred and eternal. Huzzah for us."

"HUZZAH!" cheered the peacocks.

Hampstead nodded with approval.

"Today is yet another extraordinary opportunity to do what we alone do best."

"MINGLE! GUIDE! DELIGHT!" shouted the assembly.

"Excellent!" said Hampstead. "Today's reminder: do not be stingy with your plumage. The visitors enjoy seeing your fine peacock tail feathers. Also, we apparently have a new zookeeper named Lizzie. Right. Does anyone else have business to discuss?"

Plum raised a wing.

"Anyone at all?" asked Hampstead.

Plum wiggled his wing a bit.

"Oh, fine. What is it, Plum?"

"I was thinking that it might be nice to end each visitor interaction with a cheerful farewell," said Plum.

"Not the ticking tock thing again," said Hampstead.

"No. I just thought of this one as you were speaking," said Plum. "Are you ready?"

"Enlighten us," said Hampstead.

"We could say . . . toodle pip!" shouted Plum.

There was silence.

"Mandatory Morning Meeting is adjourned," said Hampstead.

"Harrumph," he added.

Chapter Two
Jealousy, Thy Name Is Itch

The peacocks did not delight *everyone* at the Athensville Zoo, however.

If you wandered into the Small and Unusual Mammal Pavilion, past the bats and naked mole rats, you would come across this sign:

NINGBING

Cute? Maybe. But he'd make an atrocious pet!

The lone ningbing of the Athensville Zoo was named Itch. He lived up to his sign.

Did you know that a ningbing is a small marsupial that is commonly found in Western Australia? Itch knew. Itch knew many things about many animals. Itch would say that he was a genius, if you asked him.

ITCH

COMMON MOUSE

"Peacocks," spat Itch. "Why do *they* serve as ambassadors to the public? They have—quite literally—the brains of *birds*."

Itch dropped down through the tangle of branches in his cage and settled by the window. "This great zoo deserves a better guide for the visitors. An *informed* guide. I should be out there greeting the guests! I have so much knowledge to share!"

He glanced out the window. Plum was hopping along toward the new zookeeper.

"But I am contained in this cage while peacocks like Plum scamper about freely," said Itch.

The small door of Itch's cage opened. Agnes the zookeeper held out some food that had seen better days.

"Hello, my pet. Hungry?" Agnes said.

Itch ignored the question and the food. He

stared at the collection of keys attached to Agnes's belt. Her key ring also had a few cheap toys attached, including a little cartoonish mouse in short pants.

"It is time for a change at the Athensville Zoo," muttered Itch.

Outside the Small and Unusual Mammal Pavilion, Plum caught up with the new zookeeper.

"Howdy! Are you Lizzie? My name is Plum. Welcome to the Athensville Zoo family. If you have any questions—"

Lizzie stopped and looked down at the chirping peacock by her side. It seemed friendly. Almost as if it were *talking* to her.

"Hello there," said Lizzie. "And who are you?"

She leaned down and carefully reached for the tag around Plum's leg.

"Plum. What a nice name. A pleasure to meet you, Plum. I'm Lizzie. You may be the first living thing at the zoo to speak to me. It seems like a close-knit group of keepers. Being new is hard."

She smiled, then turned and entered the Small and Unusual Mammal Pavilion. The door closed

behind her. Plum stood patiently at the door. Lizzie looked back. She opened the door again.

"Do you . . . want to come in?" asked Lizzie.

Plum clucked and slipped through the door, nearly tripping Agnes.

"Cow's bells! What are you doing in here?" cried Agnes.

"Sorry, Agnes. I let Plum in," said Lizzie.

"Bad enough these peacocks are all over the

zoo. Do we have to let them *inside* now, too?"

"Well said, feed woman," Itch murmured.

"Hiya, Itch!" Plum appeared below Itch's cage.

"Plum," said Itch. "Enjoying your day?"

"Oh, yes!"

"Enjoying your duties as ambassador to the guests?"

"Yep!"

"Enjoying wasting everyone's time with pleasant greetings and cheerful frivolity?"

"Well . . . yes . . . no? I'm not wasting anyone's time, Itch."

"Hmm," said Itch. "Shall we agree to disagree?"

"Sure, I guess. See ya, Itch!"

Itch observed Plum as he hopscotched across the tiled floor behind Lizzie. Plum slipped and landed on his tail feathers.

NINGBING
CUTE? MAYBE.
BUT HE WOULD MAKE
AN ATROCIOUS PET!

"I'm okay!" said Plum, looking back at Itch with a wave.

"Okay *for now,*" said Itch.

Chapter Three
An (Almost)
Typical Day

Plum and Lizzie parted ways outside of the pavilion. She had her daily keeper duties to perform: the care and feeding of several unique and amazing animals from around the world. Plum had his own important work.

GREETING VISITORS!

RESTROOMS

HELPFUL INFO!

TODDLER RACING!

SELFIES!

Busy as he was, Plum always made time to chat with friends. Like Kevin.

Plum hopped three times and, with a bit of energetic flapping, landed on top of the statue of Plato the peacock. Now he was at eye level with the Habitrail. Kevin was fast approaching.

"Hiya, Kevin!" piped Plum.

Kevin jumped, banged his head, and slid down inside the plastic tube.

"Hi, Plum. You startled me."

"I'm sorry. I thought you saw me."

"I did," began Kevin. "But I thought you were a statue."

"I'm standing on a statue, but I'm real."

"It's hard to tell sometimes," said Kevin.

"I have actual feathers and I'm in full, glorious color." Plum spread his tail feathers.

"Where are you going?"

"Just doing laps around the zoo. I like to get in my steps," said Kevin.

"Don't let me hold you back, buddy!"

"Have a fun day, Plum!"

"Always!"

Plum flapped down and Kevin trotted off.

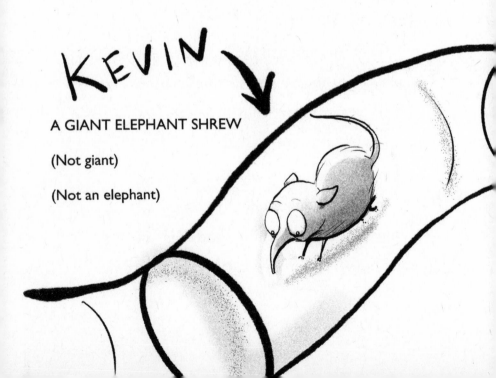

KEVIN

A GIANT ELEPHANT SHREW

(Not giant)

(Not an elephant)

The Habitrail twisted across the square, past the Prairie Dog Pound, over gift shop #6 (Monkeys & Memories), and finally through the Small and Unusual Mammal Pavilion.

"Are you going to eat that?" Kevin asked. He paused outside of Itch's cage and eyed what was left of Itch's meal.

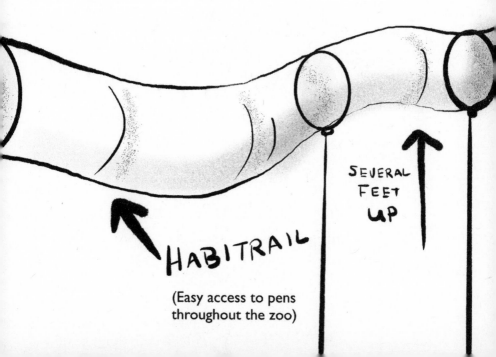

HABITRAIL

SEVERAL FEET UP

(Easy access to pens throughout the zoo)

"I'll eat *you* if you ask me that again, Kevin."

"You can't really eat me, can you? You're just a . . ." Kevin read the sign by the cage. "Ningbing. That's fun to say."

"I am glad you find it amusing," said Itch. "But to answer your question, yes. Yes, I could eat you."

Kevin gulped. "Good thing you can't get into my Habitrail."

"Oh, I can get into your Habitrail anytime I want," said Itch as he examined his nails.

"How?"

"I have my ways," said Itch.

Kevin looked around his Habitrail. It seemed safe enough.

"However, it would be unnecessary if you would simply deliver a message for me," said Itch. "A very important message."

"Um, okay," said Kevin.

"Good," said Itch. "Now listen carefully."

Itch pressed his snout to the window and whispered to Kevin.

"Is that perfectly clear?" demanded Itch.

Kevin blinked.

Itch rolled his eyes.

"Do you remember the message?"

Kevin perked up.

"Oh, yes! I remember it. It isn't clear, though."

"Fortunately, the success of phase one does not rely on your understanding. Now go, elephant shrew!"

"Okay, Itch. Bye-bye!"

Kevin zipped along the Habitrail, exiting the bungalow and scurrying across the zoo. Itch watched through his window as Kevin stopped at a point where the trail ran along the outside wall of the zoo. A large tree stood on the other side of the wall.

A squirrel appeared on a tree branch.

Then another.

Kevin said something to the squirrels.

Itch grinned his itchiest grin.

"It begins."

Plum showed off his plumage for the last visitors

as the main gate closed for the day. Turning down

the lane, he spotted the new keeper, Lizzie, alone on a bench.

"Hiya, Lizzie! How was your day? Mine was great! I—"

"Oh, hello, Plum," Lizzie said absently. "How are you? I'm off duty now. Just sitting here on a bench."

Plum hopped up beside her.

"You see that apartment building across the

street? That's where I live now. Third floor. The window without any lights on."

Plum looked. It was the only window in the building that was dark.

"This isn't just a new job. That's a new apartment. New town. I don't know anyone in Athensville yet. It's hard to meet people. For me, anyway. Animals are fine. Always have been. But people . . . that's tricky."

They sat in silence.

"Anyhoo." Lizzie stood. "I'll see you tomorrow, my fine-feathered friend."

Lizzie waved, then walked out of the zoo gates. Plum watched her cross the street and enter her building.

He waited until she turned on her light.

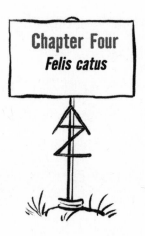

Chapter Four
Felis catus

Plum sighed and hopped off the bench. He liked the new zookeeper. He didn't like that Lizzie was lonely.

A crash snapped him out of his thoughts. A trash can had been knocked over. Hiding in the shadows, Plum could see a small, white cat with black markings. The cat didn't see Plum. It darted away. Plum followed.

The cat slinked into the thick-windowed observation hut of the lion pavilion. Plum approached the entrance.

The cat stayed by the wall. Beyond the glass, five lions lay resting. They were enormous. They were regal. They were everything a lion should be.

"Wow," gasped the wide-eyed cat.

He crept closer to the window. Closer.

The largest lion opened his eyes and swatted the glass with

a gigantic paw. The glass window shuddered and the cat bolted out of the hut, colliding with Plum. Several feathers floated gently down as cat and peacock hit the ground.

"I—I'm sorry," stammered the cat. "Are you hurt?"

Plum got back to his feet and shook his tail feathers.

"A-OK," he said.

"I was just . . ." The cat trailed off, looking back at the lion pavilion.

"King of the beasts. Impressive, right?" said Plum.

"Oh, yes!"

"You appear to be a cousin of sorts."

"No. I'm only a street cat."

"Street cat? You live in the street?"

"Well, mostly I stay at the town dump. It's not very nice. *You* get to live in the zoo. All the time!"

"Since I was a peachick!"

"That must be amazing."

"It *is*! The Athensville Zoo is the greatest place on earth!"

"I wish . . ." began the cat. He looked down. "I

should be going. You won't report me, will you?"

"Of course not. My name is Plum."

"Nice to meet you, Plum," the cat said.

Plum waited.

The cat stared blankly at Plum.

"And your name is . . ." prompted Plum.

"I don't have a name."

"Oh," said Plum. He looked at the little white cat.

"You seem like a Jeremy to me. How's that?"

The cat thought for a moment.

"Jeremy. I like it."

"Swell! Now we're friends. That's how it works. See you around, Jeremy!"

Jeremy sprang up the zoo wall, smiled at his new friend, and leaped to the street below.

Plum hummed a little tune as he meandered into the night.

Silence fell.

Then the leaves rustled in the tree outside the wall. Three squirrels watched Plum walk out of sight. Quick as a flash, they skittered down the wall and over to the entrance to the lion pavilion. Several peacock feathers lay on the ground where Plum and Jeremy had collided.

A squirrel lifted one of Plum's feathers and nodded to the others. They gathered each and every one.

**Chapter Five
Crime
Wave!**

The following day was bright and busy at the
Athensville Zoo. The sky was blue. The sun was
shining. Smiling visitors poured through the gates.

A family paused to enjoy the hippos actually
moving in their pen. The father leaned over the
rail to get a photo. His wallet protruded from his
back pocket.

A squirrel crept close along a tree branch, then lifted the wallet and replaced it with a single peacock feather.

Across the zoo, a woman sat on a bench by the carousel chatting on her phone.

A squirrel watched patiently from a nearby bush.

The woman finished her call and placed the phone beside her on the bench.

The squirrel prepared to make his move.

The woman picked up the phone again.

The squirrel settled back down.

"Annnnnd post!" murmured the woman.

She set the phone down again.

The squirrel narrowed his eyes.

"Oh!" exclaimed the woman as she scooped up her phone once more.

The squirrel slapped his tiny forehead with his tiny paw.

A boy and girl ran up to the bench.

"Mommmmmmy!" they bellowed.

"All right. All right. Just one more—"

"Noooooo!" whined the kids.

The mother put her phone down with a huff. She rifled through her pocket and held something out to her children.

"Here are some carousel tickets. Two more rides each. I'll be right there."

The kids grabbed the tickets and bolted to the carousel.

"I just have to check—"

The woman paused. Her phone was gone. She held up a single peacock feather.

Minutes later the woman joined an angry crowd at the zoo's main office. They were all shouting at once to the confused employee.

Each visitor gripped a single peacock feather.

Kevin ran down the Habitrail and skidded to a stop outside of Itch's cage.

"THE SQUIRRELS SAID—"

"Shh!" hissed Itch.

Kevin looked around the empty bungalow. He continued in a whisper.

"The squirrels said, 'Phase one complete.'"

"Perfection," Itch chortled.

"Okey dokey then!" said Kevin as he continued on his way.

Itch rubbed his little hands together.

"The peacocks will be blamed for the crime wave, and their reputation will be ruined!"

Itch rose to his full height, such as it was.

"The great Athensville Zoo will turn to the obvious choice to replace the peacocks as ambassador to all visitors . . ."

Itch raised a teeny fist in triumph.

"Me!"

At that moment, a cartoonish mouse doll in short pants smashed up against the window and startled Itch right off his branch.

"EEEEK!"

The mouse doll dangled from Agnes the zookeeper's key ring. She opened Itch's cage door.

"Sorry, little precious. Did Mommy scare you?"

Itch fumed. He boiled.

Then he reached out for the food Agnes offered.

**Chapter Six
Rogue Peacock**

The next morning, Hampstead and the peacocks gathered under the Great Tree.

"And that concludes the Mandatory Morning Meeting," intoned Hampstead. "Be safe. Be courteous. And, above all, be extraordinary. Mingle! Guide! Delight!"

"HUZZAH!" shouted the peacocks.

Plum and Meg wandered down the path together.

"Where are you going to start your day, Meg? Rhinos? Capybaras?"

"I'm not sure yet. Brrr. The air is getting chilly."

"Autumn is almost here," said Plum.

"I'll miss the crowds and warm, sunny days, but the leaves are awfully pretty," said Meg.

"They are pretty! I guess I like all of the seasons," said Plum.

"I'm not surprised, Plum. Have a nice day!" Meg smiled and walked toward the reptile house.

"I'm sure I will," said Plum. "Now, where shall I start?"

Plum began to chirp a particularly happy tune. He passed Hampstead, who was standing still as a statue, with full plumage on display.

"Stop that chirping, Plum. You sound like a common songbird."

"Songbirds are cheerful," said Plum between notes.

"Chirping is not peacock-like."

"But I'm a peacock and I chirp."

"You are the only peacock who does, Plum.

You simply must act more like the flock. Study the others and learn the proper way to behave."

"The others move too slow. I have a lot to do today, Hampstead. Peppy power!"

Plum leaped up onto a low wall and skipped

away chirping his cheerful tune.

Plum zipped across the zoo. He posed for photos. He displayed his plumage. He chatted with the bears, joked with the hyenas, and contemplated some philosophical topics with the ancient tortoises. By midday he was back at the Great Tree. The Great Tree was the hub of the peacock flock because the branches provided shade and ideal resting spots. Plum considered a short nap after his busy morning.

Suddenly Lizzie ran up to Plum.

"Plum! I'm glad I found you."

"What's up, Lizzie? You're all in a tizzy. Hey, that rhymes!"

"I tried to talk them out of it, but the keepers are rounding up the peacocks. Something about mass thievery. You need to hide!"

Lizzie picked up Plum and shoved him up into the branches of the Great Tree.

"Sorry!" said Lizzie. "I'll see if I can straighten this out. It couldn't be the peacocks. It doesn't make sense."

She darted away. Seconds later three different zookeepers herded confused peacocks past the tree. Plum spied from the safety of the branches.

"What is the meaning of this?" demanded Hampstead.

The keepers hurried Hampstead, Meg, and the rest of the peacocks along the path and out of sight.

Plum sat on a branch, deep in thought.

"Mass thievery?"

Plum glanced around himself in the Great Tree. Wallets, phones, cameras, hats, and other assorted stolen items were displayed neatly in peacock central.

"That's not good," said Plum.

As the sun set and the gates of the zoo were locked,

the peacocks found themselves in a new pen in the

back of the petting zoo. They huddled together. They whispered. They fretted.

Hampstead stood by the fence, feathers up.

"Harrumph, I say!"

And he meant it.

A sign was posted on the fence:

TEMPORARY CONTAINMENT

No Feeding. No Talking. No Looking. Really, Just Please Keep Your Distance.

This had been the least-nice day in the history of the Athensville Zoo.

Chapter Seven
Plum, PI

Plum stuck his head out from the leaves of the Great Tree. He looked left. Right. The coast was clear. Plum hopped down. He crept with caution. He stuck to the shadows. Silent. Stealthy. He pressed his feathers against the wall of the Snack Shack.

"Hundreds of animals with nothing but time

on their paws, claws, and flippers. *Someone* must have seen something!" he whispered.

Plum narrowed his eyes. "Mingle! Guide! *Interrogate!*"

First stop: the big boys.

Plum perched on the stone wall of the elephants' enclosure.

"Are you sure?" asked Plum.

"Yes." The elephant yawned.

Plum hopped onto the elephant's head.

"Nothing?"

"I saw nothing."

Plum slid down the elephant's trunk. He stared at the elephant, eye to eye.

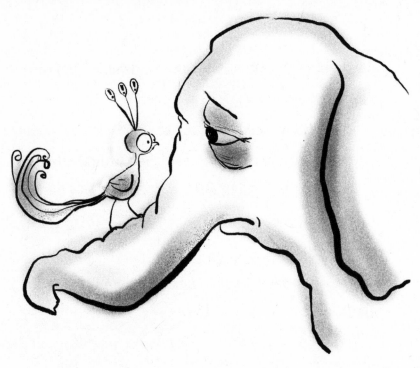

"Maybe you saw something but it slipped your mind?"

The elephant yanked his trunk out from under Plum. Plum flapped to the ground. The elephant walked away.

"Everybody forgets sometimes," mumbled Plum.

The next stop was Prairie Dog Pound. A few

prairie dogs sat in their dirt mounds chatting with Plum.

"Didn't you see *any* of the thefts?"

One of the prairie dogs vanished from the front and popped out of a hole somewhere behind Plum.

"We can't be everywhere, Plum," said the prairie dog.

Another one popped up in the corner.

"Yeah, we have our limits."

Plum stuck his head close to one of the tunnel entrances.

"But these tunnels go all over the zoo."

"Under the zoo, actually," corrected another prairie dog.

"You know what I mean," said Plum.

Several prairie dogs appeared at once and chimed in unison: "Sorry, Plum!"

"Okay. Well, keep your eye out."

"Under."

Plum wandered off into the night.

Detecting was hard work. At the beginning of the evening, Plum was sure that he would solve the mystery. But here he was, hours later, with nothing.

"It must have been an outside job," said Plum. "Maybe it was pirates?"

"Maybe," said Mike the alligator. "Probably not. You need to consider *why* someone would want to frame the peacocks."

Plum thought. Plum knew all of the animals in the zoo. He liked them. None of them would frame the peacocks.

"Nope." He shook his head. "I can't think of any animal that would do this to the peacocks even if they *had* a reason."

Plum sighed. "I guess that makes me a pretty lousy detective."

"Yes," said Mike as he slid back into the lagoon. "But it makes you a pretty great earth creature."

Plum rose slowly and dusted himself off. He needed to pep up and continue his investigation.

Maybe the lions knew something.

Chapter Eight
Tyrants

"You there!"

The voice was deep, menacing, and regal. It was, after all, a roar.

Jeremy the cat peeked out from the shadows.

The largest lion sat on his haunches behind the protective glass of the observation hut.

"Approach!"

Jeremy inched forward.

"Back again?"

Jeremy bowed his head.

"Yes, sir."

"Sir?"

Another lion joined them and pressed its muzzle against the glass by Jeremy's head.

"It's 'Your Majesty' to you!" said the second lion.

Another lion pounced down from a boulder.

"Or 'Sire'!"

And yet another lion.

"King of the beasts!"

Jeremy quaked with terror.

The largest lion relaxed and chuckled.

"Now, now, lions. I'm sure our little friend meant no disrespect."

"No, SirYourMajestySire! I have nothing but respect for lions. I mean, gosh, all cats—"

"All *cats*?" said the second lion, rising to full height.

"Is *that* what you are?" said the third lion.

"Yes," said Jeremy.

"SILENCE!" bellowed the largest lion.

The lion leaned closer to the glass and stared down at little Jeremy.

"Of course he's a cat. Look at him," said the lion.

All the lions stared intently at Jeremy. He shifted uncomfortably.

"A fine specimen of our noble breed. Are you not?" said the lion.

"I . . . I try?"

"Stand up!" commanded the lion.

Jeremy leaped to attention.

"Ears UP!"

Jeremy's ears flicked up.

"The royal bearing is evident."

Jeremy swelled with pride.

The second lion sniffed. She moved closer to the window.

"Yes. I see what you mean, Sire."

"Most impressive," added the third lion.

"A fine example," offered the fourth.

Jeremy smiled.

Plum entered the observation hut, unnoticed by the lions or Jeremy.

"And now," continued the biggest lion, "let us hear your roar."

Jeremy opened wide and let out his fiercest . . .

"MEEEEEEEOWWW!"

The lions stared.

"I am sorry. Apparently I have made a very rare error," said the lion.

The enormous lion leaned down until he was face-to-face with Jeremy, separated by the window.

"This . . . is . . . a mouse," said the lion.

The other lions chuckled.

"Or perhaps . . . a *bug*."

The lions burst into laughter.

Jeremy shrunk down.

"Certainly *not* a *cat*."

Jeremy crept out of the hut as the laughter continued. He slunk past Plum without a glance.

"Jeremy—" Plum began.

Jeremy kept going.

Plum turned. He walked up to the lions. They were still in a heap of laughter.

"Hey!" said Plum.

The lions rolled around in fits.

"HEY!" shouted Plum.

Plum's tail flew open, displaying his full breathtaking plumage. The peppy purple peacock instantly seemed three times larger.

The lions stopped laughing, gaping at the majestic tail feathers.

"*You*," said Plum, "are *not* very nice."

Plum turned and exited the hut. The lions remained silent.

His tail folded down again, Plum sped out of the lion pavilion. Jeremy was curled on a nearby bench.

"Jeremy!"

Jeremy sniffled.

"Don't listen to them," said Plum.

"They're *lions*. The big cats. I'm nothing."

"Nothing? You're a fantastic cat!"

Jeremy hopped down from the bench.

"I don't belong in the zoo. I belong in the streets."

Plum blocked his path.

"Wait. I have an idea. I'm on an investigation. I could use someone like you on my team!"

Jeremy walked around Plum.

"You're smart and stealthy. I can't even *hear* you

walking. That's perfect for detective work. You're also brave and fast! You'll be amazing! I need you!"

Jeremy turned.

"Thanks, Plum. But you're just saying that. I wouldn't be any help."

Without another word, Jeremy jumped up to a trash can, then a rooftop, then onto the wall.

"You also jump really well!" called Plum.

Jeremy slipped over the wall and out of the zoo.

Plum sighed, alone in the dark.

The lions had surprised him. Why be so mean to Jeremy? But they *had* been mean. He had seen it. Could other animals also surprise him?

And did that mean that there *could* be someone in the zoo who wanted the peacocks rounded up?

This sad thought took the pep right out of Plum's step.

**Chapter Nine
Phase 1-A**

The next day Itch sat staring through his window. In the far corner of the zoo grounds, he could see a sliver of the temporary peacock pen.

"Why are those blasted birds still here?"

He hopped to a new branch.

"All evidence points to their guilt! The logical action is to get rid of them, not keep them in a little pen!"

He hung upside down.

"Humans!"

Elsewhere, Kevin woke from a nap in the capybara pen. He took a bite of some food, then entered his Habitrail, waving to the capybara.

"See ya, Cap!"

Kevin jogged along the trail, humming to himself, until he was above the penned-in peacocks. He looked down at them, his merry hum trailing off. He waved sadly before continuing down the Habitrail.

A squirrel sat on a low branch just outside the zoo wall.

Kevin eyed the squirrel and scurried past.

His Habitrail ran alongside a group of zookeepers who were on their morning rounds.

Kevin noticed the nice new one, Lizzie.

"Oh, I guess we'll keep the peacocks in for another day or so," said the first zookeeper.

"At least until we clear this up," said a second.

"You don't really suppose the peacocks could be responsible for the thefts?"

"It doesn't seem right."

Lizzie, who hadn't spoken yet, couldn't stay quiet any longer.

"Of course it doesn't seem right! Why would the peacocks steal from our visitors? The peacocks are friendly. They're not crooks."

Kevin continued on. He entered the Small and Unusual Mammal Pavilion. Itch stopped him as he passed.

"Report, Kevin! What is going on? Why are the peacocks still here?" demanded Itch.

Kevin backed up against his Habitrail to keep the maximum distance from Itch's window. Then he told him what the zookeepers had said.

"They are hesitating," said Itch as he snapped a twig.

"*You* don't think the peacocks stole all of those things, do you, Itch?" asked Kevin.

Itch glared at him sideways.

"One day soon I shall lecture the guests about the remarkable brain of the elephant shrew."

Kevin's eyes widened. "Thanks!"

"It was not a compliment. Scurry, Kevin. I must think."

Kevin scurried down the Habitrail.

Itch thought. And after a few moments, he smiled.

"Very well. I shall take matters into my own capable hands. Time to initiate phase one-A!"

Agnes and another zookeeper entered the bungalow with feed pails.

"All I'm saying is that I think those birds had a bit too much freedom," grumbled Agnes.

"They did seem to be everywhere at once," said the other zookeeper.

Agnes opened Itch's cage door.

Itch stared from the corner of his cage.

Agnes tossed Itch's food into the cage. When she turned away, the key chain on her belt jingled by the small open door.

"Everywhere at once is right," said Agnes. "And those feathers were found at the scenes. What other explanation is there?"

Agnes shut the door.

"I can't believe the on-duty zookeepers didn't see anything," continued Agnes. "*I* would have noticed something, I'll tell you that."

She picked up her feed bucket and headed out of the bungalow.

Back in Itch's cage, the toy mouse from Agnes's key ring sat perched on a branch.

The key ring on Agnes's hip swung with each step. Itch clung to the ring in the doll's place.

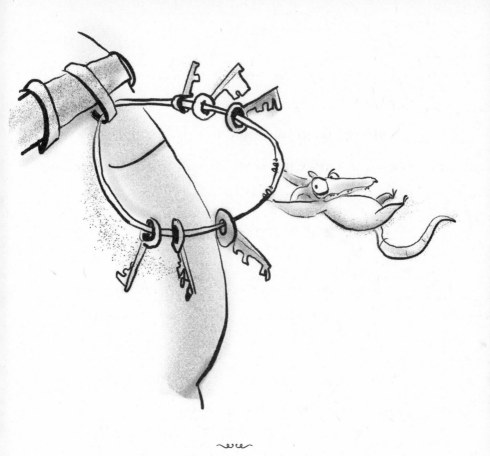

Plum sat in the Great Tree, where he had remained hidden all day. He looked at the stolen goods still stashed in the branches. He was no closer to solving the mystery.

When evening came and the zoo was closed

and deserted, Plum plopped down to the ground.

He took a deep breath.

"I can't give up," said Plum. "I might not have the answers, I might not be a great detective, but I can still try to cheer up my friends. There's always hope."

Plum made his way to the new peacock pen. But he did not chirp, not even quietly.

Chapter Ten
Peacock Pokey

Tension was high among the peacocks. A full day and a half without mingling, guiding, or delighting had affected each and every one of them.

"I can't take it anymore. I can't!"

"Get a grip, Charles," said one peacock.

"Stiff upper beak and all that," chirped a second.

"We *are* peacocks, after all," pointed out a third.

"Are we?" said Hampstead. He was lying in the corner.

He stood and stomped to the center.

"Look at us. Suspected. Caged. Reduced in stature and duty."

Hampstead slumped back down.

"We are nothing but guinea hens."

"I don't even know what those are," said another peacock.

"It is all over," moaned Hampstead.

"Don't forget that Plum is still out there," said Meg.

"*Plum!*" Hampstead snorted.

"Did someone bellow my name?" Plum skipped up to the gate.

"Plum!" said Meg. "Did they find the real thieves? Are we going to be released?"

"Wellllll . . . ," began Plum.

"Yes?" said the peacocks eagerly.

"No," said Plum.

The peacocks drooped.

"But I'm sure it will be all right . . . eventually," said Plum. "In the meantime, I am here to cheer you up!"

"This is my worst nightmare," said Hampstead.

"Knock-knock," said Plum brightly.

"Do you hear something?" asked Meg.

"You're supposed to say 'Who's there?'" said Plum.

"No, Plum," continued Meg. "That . . . *scurrying* sound."

Scrittle

   Scrittle

      Scrittle

The peacocks huddled together, feathers trembling.

Plum stood at the gate, wings and tail outstretched.

A gang of squirrels scampered out of the shadows and surrounded the peacock pen.

One squirrel leaped to the front. Itch was riding on his back.

"I did not see that coming," admitted Plum.

"PEACOCKS! Listen well!" shouted Itch.

"Itch, what are you doing outside?" asked Plum.

"I said 'listen,' not 'talk'! I was very, very clear!"

A squirrel growled at Plum. If you have never heard a squirrel growl, you are lucky.

"Peacocks, your reign of terror is at an end," continued Itch.

The peacocks exchanged looks with one another.

"No longer are you the free-range ambassadors of the Athensville Zoo!"

Itch paused to relish the moment.

"From this night forward, I, Itch the rare and unusual NINGBING, shall be engaging the visitors of the finest zoo in the world. ASSEMBLE (in an orderly fashion)! LECTURE! ENLIGHTEN!"

Itch climbed down from his squirrel's back.

"If your minuscule brains can manage," he continued, "imagine the possibilities. . . .

"Regularly scheduled lectures hosted by me! Knowledge without glitz, glamour, or gimmicks!

"Slide shows! No . . . PowerPoint!

"Mandatory educational opportunities at every bend. Well-behaved animals presented in a clear, factual manner!

"Pop quizzes!" Itch took a deep breath.

"Well? What do you say about that?" demanded Itch.

"Sounds a bit dull," offered one peacock.

"Yes. Lacking in amusement entirely," said a peahen.

"More like school than a zoo," said another.

"Peacocks!" spat Itch. He hopped back onto the squirrel. "So superior with your plumage. So above it all. Well, we'll see how you really feel *above it all*!"

The peacocks stared blankly.

"I'm sorry, Itch," said Plum. "You've lost us again."

"I should have saved that for later," muttered Itch. "Arrgh! No matter."

A squirrel unlatched the gate.

"MARCH!" commanded Itch.

The squirrels herded the peacocks down the darkened path.

Meg and Plum walked together.

"Plum, what is he going to do to us?" whispered Meg.

"Hard to say. He seems a little excited," said Plum.

"We need to escape somehow," said Meg.

A boarded-up staircase loomed ahead.

"There's nothing here except for . . ." Plum trailed off with a gulp.

They stopped. All of the peacocks looked up.

High above them, creaking and ancient, loomed the dilapidated monorail station, with its rusted elevated track. A sign by the staircase read:

KIDDIE MONORAIL!

A View from Above!

Fun AND Safe!

That sign had been plastered with more recent notices:

UNSAFE!

BEWARE!

NO ENTRY!

BAD MONORAIL!

"This is not good," said Plum.

Chapter Eleven
Danger!
Rickety!

Up on the monorail platform, the squirrels shoved the peacocks into the ancient kiddie rail car.

"This is an outrage!" sputtered Hampstead at the squirrels guarding the door.

Itch stood on the old control panel, a rusted lever by his paw.

"This is a revolution!" shouted Itch.

"You're bananas!" said Meg.

"Am I? I'm going to throw this switch and send you peacocks circling above the zoo *forever*! Is that bananas?"

"Actually, it is sort of bananas, Itch," said Plum.

"Or . . ."—Itch paused—"or until the monorail crashes to your doom!"

"That seems more likely," admitted Plum.

He looked down. They were indeed very high up.

"You know, Itch," Plum began, "there must be another way. We're all friends—"

"We are *not* friends, Plum!" shouted Itch. "We are competitors. I am simply removing my competition."

The monorail swayed and creaked.

And *creaked*.

"Good-bye, you fine-feathered yet inadequate guides," said Itch.

Itch tried to throw the lever, but it was rusted and stuck. He climbed up and stomped on it. It didn't budge.

"Help me!"

A couple of squirrels snapped to attention and bolted over to assist Itch. The lever shifted to On.

The monorail rumbled. It trembled. And then it began to wobble down the track. The peacocks clung together in the tiny car. All was silent inside the monorail. And then . . .

"AHHHHHHHHHHH!!!" The peacocks jumped and flapped and squawked in terror.

The monorail swayed even more. The dim light inside the car flickered on and off, making a *zzzt* sound.

"Stop it, everyone!" Meg stood up on a seat. "We're making it worse! We must remain calm. There's always a solution. Right, Plum?"

All eyes turned to Plum, who was slumped in a seat by a window.

"Plum?" asked Meg again quietly.

"I . . . I don't know," said Plum.

"For once, he's right," said Hampstead. "No one can save us."

Plum stared out the window. As the monorail turned a corner on its track, the town dump came into view beyond the zoo's wall.

Plum leaped up onto his seat, full of pep.

"Hold it! Forget what I said! And definitely forget what Hampstead said! Everyone start squawking and shake the monorail again!"

"WHAT?" demanded Hampstead.

Meg started jumping up and down.

"Trust Plum," she shouted. "Come on, everybody. Let's rock this boat!"

And the peacocks did—with enthusiasm. The monorail swayed from side to side. The light blinked on and off, on and off, on and off.

Plum looked out toward the town dump as the monorail slowly passed. He pressed his wing against the window and hoped with all his might.

Chapter Twelve
A Friend in Need

Watching the shaking monorail, Itch cackled in triumph.

But far below in the dark zoo, a white streak dashed over the wall, passed the lion hut, and sped toward the monorail steps.

It was Jeremy.

He leaped once, twice, three times, and he

was there in the control booth!

Itch and the squirrels let out startled squeaks.

"Who are you?" demanded Itch.

"I am a cat. I am brave, I am fast, *and* I can jump really well!"

Jeremy hissed with all his might, his tail sticking out straight and fuzzy.

The squirrels bolted.

Jeremy pinned Itch with one paw and pulled the lever with another. The monorail creaked to a stop.

"My name is Jeremy. And Plum is *my friend*!"

Itch glared.

Jeremy threw the lever into reverse. The monorail backed up slowly. As soon as it had returned safely to the station platform, the peacocks piled out.

"Jeremy! You're a king among cats!" said Plum.
"I knew you would come!"

Jeremy grinned. "That's what friends are for,
Plum."

Itch squirmed under Jeremy's paw.

"What should we do with Itch?" asked Meg.

"We need to return him to the Small and Unusual Mammal Pavilion," said Hampstead. "But the doors will be locked."

"We'll have to take him to a place that isn't locked," said Plum. "I have an idea, but we'll need something to keep Itch there until morning."

"What?" asked Hampstead.

"Well," began Plum, "this might not be the proper way for a peacock to behave, and it certainly isn't dignified. But I know where we can find something that will keep Itch in place for the night."

Hampstead looked at another peacock. The peacock shrugged.

"All right, Plum," said Hampstead. "What do we do?"

The peacocks scoured the dark zoo. They looked under picnic tables and behind benches.

Hampstead spotted his quarry: a lump of gum stuck under a bench. He clawed and pecked at the gum.

"Harrumph," muttered Hampstead to himself.

Morning finally arrived at the Athensville Zoo. A group of zookeepers gathered in the lions' observation hut. They stared at the window.

"Well whaddaya know about that?"

Itch was stuck to the glass with bits of chewing gum and gummy worms. The stolen goods were

piled on the floor beneath him, along with a single peacock feather.

"Grrr" was all that Itch could manage.

On the other side of the glass, the lions stared at Itch's tiny bottom pressed against the window.

"Is someone going to clean this up?" asked the king of beasts. "Umm . . . please?"

After Itch was returned to his cage in the Small and Unusual Mammal Pavilion, his sign was changed to read:

VERY NAUGHTY

DO NOT TRUST!

BAD NINGBING!

Later that day, Plum spotted Jeremy hopping onto the wall. Plum rushed up to him.

"Jeremy! Wait!"

Jeremy paused.

"There's someone I'd very much like you to meet," said Plum.

Moments later the small white cat with black markings walked cautiously up to Lizzie the zookeeper. Lizzie looked at the cat. She bent down. The cat walked close enough for her to pet him. She did. He purred.

"You look like a Jeremy to me," she said.

Chapter Thirteen
All's Well at the Athensville Zoo

Plum waited at the door to the Small and Unusual Mammal Pavilion. He had one more task to perform.

Eventually Agnes the keeper opened the door. Plum scurried in before she could stop him.

"Hey," said Agnes. "Get back here!"

Plum skidded to a stop in front of Itch's cage.

Agnes approached, and for the first time noticed that Plum held a brochure in his beak. He seemed to want her to have it.

Agnes took the brochure and read the cover.

*Book the **TRAVELING ATHENSVILLE ZOO** for your school or library!*

EDUCATIONAL!

FASCINATING!

LIVE ANIMALS!

and

LECTURES!

She looked back at Plum. Plum tipped his head toward Itch.

"Hmm," said Agnes. She showed Itch the brochure.

Itch read the brochure cover and then read it again with excitement. He pressed his face against the cage and watched as Plum made his way to the door.

Plum turned, smiled, and waved.

Itch waved back.

The sun began to set.

Plum strolled the grounds with Meg. Other peacocks mingled with the last guests of the day as they filed out of the zoo.

"All's well that ends well," said Plum.

"It all has ended well, hasn't it?" said Meg.

Lizzie walked by on her way out of the gate.

"Good night, you two," said Lizzie.

Meg and Plum watched Lizzie cross the street and head toward her apartment building.

Inside the apartment, Jeremy's eyes flicked open.

He leaped to a carpet—

Bounded to a chair—

Swiped a paw at the chain of a lamp—

And turned on the light.

Lizzie paused on the sidewalk. She looked up to her apartment. Her window was the only one with a light on.

Jeremy hopped onto the windowsill.

Lizzie laughed and blew him a little kiss.

"You are a wonder, Plum," said Meg. She began to walk down the path, paused, and turned back.

"Toodle pip!" said Meg.

"And toodle pip to you, my friend!" said Plum.

Plum made his way across the Athensville Zoo in the golden twilight. He chirped a peppy little tune, looking forward to tomorrow.

Plum and his friends are going to school—in a blizzard! Read on for a sneak peek!

A SNOW DAY FOR

PLUM!

THE SEQUEL TO *LEAVE IT TO PLUM!*

MATT PHELAN

Plum and his friends are going to school—in a blizzard! Read on for a sneak peek!

A SNOW DAY FOR

PLUM!

THE SEQUEL TO *LEAVE IT TO PLUM!*

MATT PHELAN

Chapter One
The Traveling Athensville Zoo

Plum the peacock sat still and quiet. He was usually pretty peppy. His friends at the Athensville Zoo would say he was cheerful and chatty. But this morning, Plum did not feel like his usual peppy, cheerful, chatty self. Plum felt a little bit—just a little bit—scared.

"Isn't this exciting?" asked Meg.

Plum and Meg sat in individual peacock cages. Next to them were cages that contained Kevin, a giant elephant shrew (not giant, nor an elephant); Jeremy, a former street cat, now happily owned by Lizzie the zookeeper; Myrna, a colorful parrot; and Itch, a ningbing (small mammal, unusual in many ways).

"'Exciting' is too mild a word," said Itch. "'Thrilling,' perhaps. Is there a word that aptly describes the sensation of fulfilling one's destiny?"

"Nausea?" asked Kevin, who was feeling a little wobbly in the belly.

You see, these fine animals of the Athensville

Zoo were not, in fact, at the zoo. They were bouncing along in the back of a zoo van. They were on their way to visit Romeburg Elementary School.

"Just think," said Itch, "in less than an hour, I shall be lecturing eager young minds about the great wonders of the animal kingdom!"

"I think Lizzie is actually doing the lecturing part," said Meg.

"Perhaps—dare I dream?—I will use the SMART Board!" said Itch, ignoring Meg.

"Maybe the visit will be canceled," said Plum in a small voice.

"Canceled?" said Itch. "Why on earth would it be canceled?"

"Well," said Plum a bit louder, "I think the school might soon be buried in snow."

~eve~